D1405158

The Nine Days Wonder

MARILYN HOLLINSHEAD
with pictures by **PIERR MORGAN**

PHILOMEL BOOKS
NEW YORK

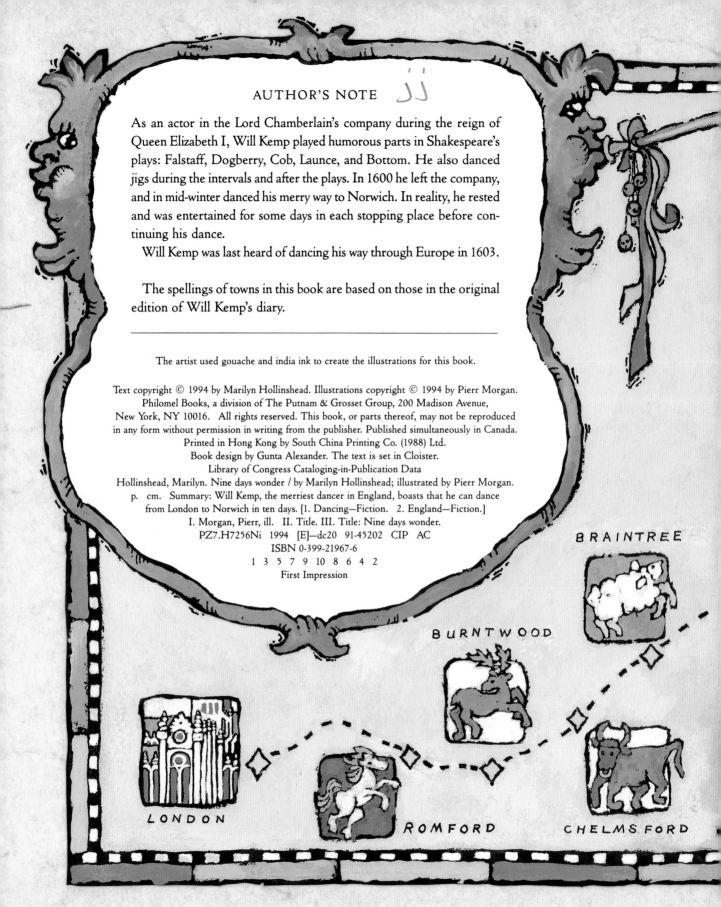

AUTHOR'S NOTE

As an actor in the Lord Chamberlain's company during the reign of Queen Elizabeth I, Will Kemp played humorous parts in Shakespeare's plays: Falstaff, Dogberry, Cob, Launce, and Bottom. He also danced jigs during the intervals and after the plays. In 1600 he left the company, and in mid-winter danced his merry way to Norwich. In reality, he rested and was entertained for some days in each stopping place before continuing his dance.

Will Kemp was last heard of dancing his way through Europe in 1603.

The spellings of towns in this book are based on those in the original edition of Will Kemp's diary.

The artist used gouache and india ink to create the illustrations for this book.

Book design by Gunta Alexander. The text is set in Cloister.
Library of Congress Cataloging-in-Publication Data
Hollinshead, Marilyn. Nine days wonder / by Marilyn Hollinshead; illustrated by Pierr Morgan.
p. cm. Summary: Will Kemp, the merriest dancer in England, boasts that he can dance from London to Norwich in ten days. [1. Dancing—Fiction. 2. England—Fiction.]
I. Morgan, Pierr, ill. II. Title. III. Title: Nine days wonder.
PZ7.H7256Ni 1994 [E]—dc20 91-45202 CIP AC
ISBN 0-399-21967-6
1 3 5 7 9 10 8 6 4 2
First Impression

BRAINTREE

BURNTWOOD

LONDON

ROMFORD

CHELMSFORD

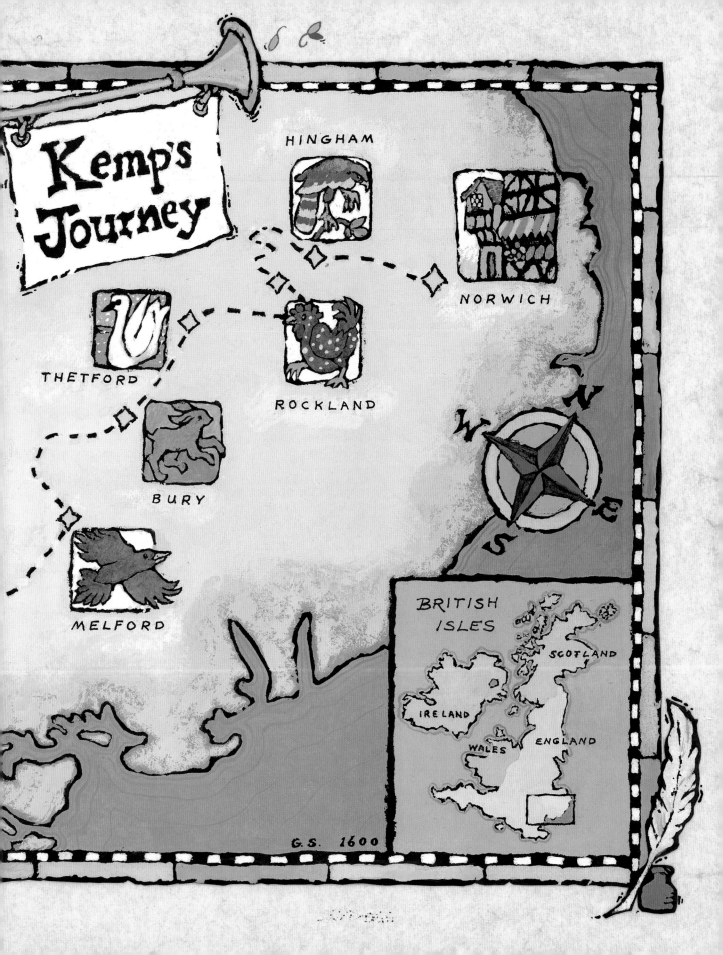

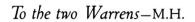

The merriest dancer in all England was Will Kemp. He loved to dance in grand houses or in the streets of London. He loved to dance a jig at the end of a play and to dance at country fairs.

Will loved to dance so much that one day he boasted, "I can dance in wind and weather all the way from London to Norwich."

No one can dance that far, everyone said. Norwich was one hundred and seventeen miles away! Walking, yes, but dancing, never.

They all placed bets that Will couldn't do it.

Will only laughed. "I'll dance it in ten days or less, and sleep only at night." He was sure that he could do it.

So early on a winter morning Will stood at the Lord Mayor of London's house with his servant Will Bee, George Sprat, the mile keeper, and friend Tom Slye, who merrily struck up the drums. And off leaped Will, dancing nonny-nonny right through London and into the countryside.

"I'll stop at nothing," Will said.

He refused to stop for a bearbaiting, although he could hear the bear roar.

He refused to sip from a great spoon, although the drink smelled delightsome.

He refused to stop when the sun went down, and danced on by moonshine.

But then, tripping down a narrow road, two fighting horses blocked his way.

"Can I make it?" thought Will, but skimble-skamble he danced right under the two horses' legs.

No wonder he decided it was time to rest in Romford at the end
of the first day's dance.

The next day, earlier than the lark, Will heard Tom Slye piping
a lively tune, and at the place where Will had stopped his dance
he tripped lightly forward.

But he felt a pain in his hip.

"If this came from a turn in my dancing," he said, "by dancing I'll turn it out again."

So lippity-loppity, turn he did, through copses and hamlets and over hills to Burntwood, until the pain was gone.

"It's certain I can do it," said Will.

"This pain can come back," said George Sprat.

On the third day a spry young maid begged to dance with Will, and with bells ringing they hotfooted the hills and the hall of one great house together.

Then Will tripped it alone to Chelmsford.
"Too much dilly dallying," said George Sprat.

On the fourth morning Will found the road full of muck. He sang,
 "With hey and ho through thick and thin,
 The hobbyhorse quite forgotten,
 I followed, as I did begin,
 Although the way were rotten."

And down the lane he slogged, followed by two hobbledehoy country boys. But when Will jumped a broad puddle, one boy took the same jump and landed in the middle.

Will laughed and danced on. "I can do it," sang Will.

"You are tiring fast," said George Sprat.

On the fifth day Will capered out of Braintree with a brawny butcher, but the butcher soon gave up.

"That's a fainthearted lout," called a plump country lass. "I'll tread one mile with Master Kemp myself."

Her swig-a-swag dance made crowds laugh, but it was a tired
Will who rested that night at a gentleman's house in Melford.
"Just as I thought," hummed George Sprat.
But Will Kemp was halfway.

On the sixth day Will bounded tripping and twirling to Bury.
Just as he capered through one of Bury's town gates, there arrived
at the other gate the Lord Chief Justice.

But the streets were empty for the Lord Chief Justice. Instead the crowds thronged around Will.

Will was weary that night from dancing all day. He was weary
from leaping through puddles and muck. He was weary from
struggling through crowds. And he still had three more days to go.

"Can I really do it?" sighed Will.

"I don't think so," smiled George Sprat.

On the seventh day it snowed. It snowed and it snowed, great
feathery flakes. Even so, Will set out, feather-heeled, and danced
ten miles to Thetford.

That night George Sprat was silent.

On the eighth day Will found the road to Rockland full of ruts, and full of people crowding around him. At each crossroads people cried out,

"This way is the nearest!"

"The fairest way is through our village!"

"Take the next turn on the left."

It made Will's head spin, so he danced higgledy-piggledy down

the rough road, turning this way and that until finally he reached Hingham.

The eighth day was over. And he was only one day from Norwich.

"It's not over yet," scowled George Sprat.

When Will danced his hey-de-gay onward the next morning, his pace was so lively that five young men had to run to keep up.

Dancing up a rise, Will saw the city of Norwich at last. He also saw problems and sent a message to the Lord Mayor there.

There were little gates across the streets, Will said. So the Lord Mayor had the gates removed.

There were too many people for a merry morris dancer, Will said. So the Lord Mayor hired wifflers with sticks to keep the crowds back.

Then in fine fettle Will danced through St. Stephen's Gate right into the market place.

On the market cross the city musicians sang to him. But with a hey-nonny-nonny Will danced on.

He leaped through the crowd and landed on a young girl's skirt. Off came her petticoat, but Will couldn't tarry to help her.

The crowds were now as thick as clotted cream.

"I'll never make it at this dib-a-dab pace," he thought.

So Will leaped a wall into a churchyard, leaving behind not only the crowds but his servant Will Bee, his taborer Tom Slye, and his mile keeper, George Sprat.

Will twirled through the tombstones and leaped over the church gate. With a roar the people ran after him, but, ahead of them all, Will danced jig-a-jog right up to the house of the Lord Mayor of Norwich.

Will had danced one hundred and seventeen miles in just nine days!

As the people cheered, Will celebrated with a great leap.

"Hurray," said Will. "I can collect my winnings. I danced the whole way."

But George Sprat stepped forward with book and quill.

"Nay," he said. "I saw you not after you leaped into the churchyard. I know not whether you danced—or walked—that distance."

"Heigh-ho," Will said. "Then I'll trip the distance with you again, George Sprat."

So back to the church they went, and outside the churchyard this time, Will danced tilly-fally to the Lord Mayor's house again.

Finally George Sprat was satisfied.

Will rode to London to collect his winnings.

He was famous. Everyone was writing or talking about his long dance.

But for a little while, Will stopped his hey-de-gay dancing, just long enough to write a book about his journey. He called it *Kemp's Nine Days Wonder*.

"Now, I'll dance myself out into the world," said Will.